This book belongs to:

....

....

For my lovely primary school teacher Jenny Langman –
thank you for being such an inspiration xx

Quarto is the authority on a wide range of topics.

Quarto educates, entertains and enriches the lives of
our readers—enthusiasts and lovers of hands-on living.

www.quartoknows.com

Author and illustrator: Lucy Barnard
Designer: Victoria Kimonidou
Editor: Ellie Brough

Part of The Quarto Group
The Old Brewery
6 Blundell Street
London N7 9BH

A catalogue record for this book is available from
the British Library.

ISBN 978 1 78493 939 7

Printed in China

MIX
Paper from
responsible sources
FSC® C016973

I'm Bigger than You!

by LUCY BARNARD

George loved reminding his sister Lottie that he was bigger than her.

"You can't use pens, you need to use your crayons."

"You have to use your beaker or you'll spill your drink."

He was always reminding Lottie that he was her big brother.

"I'll win this race because I'm much bigger than you."

"I don't need to stand on the step because I can reach without it."

"Just because I'm smaller than you, doesn't mean I'm a baby," said Lottie crossly.

"Now, now," said Mummy. "No arguing please, or Daddy and I won't take you to the fairground later."

George and Lottie jumped
up and down with excitement.

THE FAIRGROUND!

At the fairground George and Lottie whizzed down the helter-skelter.

WEEEEEE!

They crashed into each other in the dodgem cars.

BASH!

BUMP!

HOORAY!

They hooked ducks and each won a toy.

On the big wheel Lottie held
on tightly to Mummy.

"I don't need to hold onto
you Daddy," said George.
"I'm too big to be scared."

They were just getting all sticky with candyfloss when George saw the most amazing ride ever, the super-duper **BIG DIPPER** rollercoaster!

"I'm definitely going on that but you're too small Lottie," announced George.

YOU NEED TO BE THIS BIG TO RIDE

The rollercoaster was **bumpy** and **shaky**.

It went so fast it made George's tummy flip over like a pancake.

When the ride had stopped George climbed out
with very shaky legs and stumbled over to Mummy.

"Oh George," she said, "that was
a bit too **much** for you wasn't it?"

"See," said Lottie, "I'm not the
only one too small for that ride."

Later on, George didn't even argue when he had to go to bed at the same time as Lottie.

"Don't be sad," said Mummy. "There are some things you aren't quite ready for yet and some things that you may never be ready for."

"Daddy's bigger than all of us but he's still scared of spiders!" she said. George and Lottie both giggled.

Just then, Daddy poked his head round the door. "I have a very important question. Is anyone here too big for hot chocolate and cuddles?"

"**NO!**" shouted Mummy, George and Lottie all together.

George was very happy that there are some things you're never too big for!

NEXT STEPS

Discussion and Comprehension

Ask the children the following questions and discuss their answers.

- What did you like most about this story?
- How do you think Lottie felt when George kept saying he was bigger than her?
- What was Daddy scared of?
- Who is the biggest in your family?

Learn about Suffixes (est)

George was always reminding Lottie that he was her *big* brother. Explain that he is *bigger* than Lottie, but he isn't the *biggest* in the family. Ask the children to look at the characters and say who they think is the biggest. Model the following two sentences: 'Daddy is big.' 'Daddy is the biggest.' Explain that 'big' is an adjective and 'est' is a suffix. Ask the children which character they think is the youngest, smallest, tallest, oldest, kindest and so on. Ask them to choose one of these adjectives and write two sentences in the same format as the modelled sentences.

Happy Face, Sad Face

Give the children two large paper plates, coloured felt pens, brown wool, safety scissors and glue. Ask them to make one picture of George's face when Mummy told him that they were going to the fairground and one of George's face after he came off the rollercoaster. Ask them to explain their work and discuss the emotions they have presented.